Acknowledgment
Special thanks to Janet Robinson of Young Explorers Ltd, Leicester.

British Library Cataloguing in Publication Data
Where's Rudolph?
   I. Burton, Terry   II. Series
   823'.914 [J]
   ISBN 0-7214-9610-5

First edition

Published by Ladybird Books Ltd Loughborough Leicestershire UK
Ladybird Books Inc Auburn Maine 04210 USA
Printed in England

Where's Rudolph?

illustrated by Terry Burton

Ladybird Books

It was Christmas Eve, time for Santa Claus to set off on his journey round the world.

Santa had his list of names and addresses. He knew where there were blocked-up chimneys or slippery roofs, and he knew which children were away from home.

The elves had packed up all the presents and loaded them onto the sleigh.

And the reindeer were lined up and ready to go—all except Rudolph, the reindeer whose shining red nose always showed Santa the way.

No! It's an elf mending the roof.

Is Rudolph in there?

Is Rudolph in there?

No! It's just an elf putting the car away.

No! It's the carol singers' lantern.

Is that Rudolph?

No! It's an elf trying on his clown costume for the party.

Could that be Rudolph?

No! It's a bowl of bright red apples.

Is that Rudolph?

No! The elves and animals are playing ball.

Did *anyone* find Rudolph?

"Yes!" said Santa Claus. "I did! He was polishing his nose so it would shine extra bright to guide us on our way tonight!"